CW01073061

Mystery Valentine

A boy was sitting on the ledge inside the fireplace, a boy of about her own age. He was sitting very still – his thin arms hugging his knees, which were drawn up under his chin – and he was watching her.

"Oh!" Sophie gasped. "You made me jump. Who are you?" she said when he didn't move. "What are you doing there?"

He didn't answer immediately, just carried on staring at Sophie with dark, sad eyes.

Dare you try *another* Young Hippo Spooky?

Ghost Dog
Eleanor Allen

The Screaming Demon Ghostie
Jean Chapman

The Green Hand
Tessa Krailing

Smoke Cat
Linda Newbery

Bumps in the Night
Frank Rodgers

The Kings' Castle
Ann Ruffell

Scarem's House
Malcolm Yorke

What about a fantastic Young Hippo Magic story?

My Friend's a Gris-Quok!
Malorie Blackman

Diggory and the Boa Conductor
The Little Pet Dragon
Philippa Gregory

Broomstick Services
Ann Jungman

Hello Nellie and the Dragon
Elizabeth Lindsay

The Marmalade Pony
Linda Newbery

Mr Wellington Boots
Ann Ruffell

The Wishing Horse
Malcolm Yorke

CAROL BARTON

Mystery
Valentine

Illustrated by Jan Lewis

For Daniel

Scholastic Children's Books,
Commonwealth House, 1-19 New Oxford Street,
London WC1A 1NU, UK
a division of Scholastic Ltd
London ~ New York ~ Toronto ~ Sydney ~ Auckland

Published in the UK by Scholastic Ltd, 1997

Text copyright © Carol Barton, 1997
Illustrations copyright © Jan Lewis, 1997

ISBN 0 590 13925 8

Typeset by Backup Creative Services, Dorset
Printed by Cox & Wyman Ltd, Reading, Berks

10 9 8 7 6 5 4 3 2 1

All rights reserved

The rights of Carol Barton and Jan Lewis to be identified respectively
as the author and illustrator of this work have been asserted by them in
accordance with the Copyright, Designs and Patents Act, 1988.

This book is sold subject to the condition that it shall not, by way of trade or
otherwise, be lent, resold, hired out, or otherwise circulated without the
publisher's prior consent in any form of binding or cover other than that in
which it is published and without a similar condition, including this condition,
being imposed upon the subsequent purchaser.

Chapter 1

"Is this where you live?" Alice Jupe stepped off the school bus and turned to Sophie, her mouth falling open in surprise. When Sophie nodded in reply Alice said, "But it's so big."

"It's an old manor house," said Sophie.

"But why do you need such a big house? Have you got lots of brothers and sisters?"

"No," said Sophie, then wistfully added, "there's only me… and Mummy and Daddy of course. Daddy's a potter," she went on as they began to walk up the gravel drive to the big house, "and Mummy is an artist. They are going to open a craft centre – there will be lots of other people working here then."

"Is that why you came to the Isle of Wight to live?" asked Alice curiously.

Sophie nodded then turned and saw that her friend had stopped and was looking up at the house. Great black rooks cawed noisily from the branches of the tall trees that lined the drive, and even as the two girls watched the birds began to circle the house's many chimneys.

"Is there a ghost?" asked Alice after a moment.

"Ghost?" Sophie was startled. "I don't think so," she said. "Why?"

"Oh, it must have a ghost," said Alice importantly. "My mother says all old manor houses are haunted."

At that moment the front door opened and Sophie's mother appeared. She was wearing a dark blue flowered dress that reached her ankles, and a fawn cardigan.

Her dark hair was long, like Sophie's, and she had the same brown eyes.

"Hello, darling," she said to Sophie. "Had a good day?"

Sophie nodded. "This is my friend, Alice. You said she could come to tea."

"I certainly did. Hello, Alice. Come on inside, we'll go into the kitchen. It's warm in there – and quiet!" She glanced up at the sky. "Those rooks have been making that dreadful racket all day. So what have you been doing at school today?" she called over her shoulder as they made their way down a dark passage.

"We've been learning about Saint Valentine," said Sophie. As they reached the kitchen the warmth from a large, black stove hit their cold cheeks.

"It's Saint Valentine's Day on Saturday." Mum took a batch of scones from the stove. "Oh, that's hot!" she exclaimed, hastily dropping the tray on to the kitchen table.

"We've been making cards to send to our valentines," said Alice. "I shall send mine to Jason Biddleton. Who is your valentine, Sophie?"

"I haven't got one," said Sophie with a shrug.

"Never mind." Sophie's mum smiled and tipped a couple of scones on to a plate before handing them to the two girls. "The main thing is, have you had fun making the cards?"

"Oh, yes," said Sophie.

"I think those rooks must know it's nearly Valentine's Day," said Mum, "they've been pairing up for days now. Daddy is afraid they'll build their nests in the chimney pots."

"Are we going to have a fire in the inglenook fireplace?" Sophie spread butter on to her scone and bit into it.

"Well, we hope to…" Mum turned back to the stove.

"What's an inglenook?" asked Alice.

"I'll show you," said Sophie, wiping butter from her chin, and feeling secretly pleased that there seemed to be something her new friend didn't know. "Come on, it's in the dining room." Still munching her scone she led the way out of the kitchen and back down the dark passage to the hall, where she pushed open another door.

The room they entered was cold but bright, with pale winter sunshine streaming through the big windows.

"There's the inglenook," said Sophie, pointing to the far end of the room. Then as Alice turned she led the way to the big stone fireplace.

"Look," she said, "you can step right inside and see up the chimney."

Alice followed her into the inglenook and the pair of them peered up the dark tunnel.

"I don't like it," said Alice. "It's creepy." She stepped back into the room.

"Well, you said you wanted to see it," protested Sophie.

"So what else have you got to show me?" Alice began to walk down the room again to the door.

"You can come and see the old stables if you like." Sophie stepped out of the fireplace.

"Do you have horses?" asked Alice eagerly.

"No." Sophie shook her head. "I wish we did."

"So what's the point in going to the stables?"

"It's where Daddy has his pottery. It's great fun watching him at his wheel—" Sophie broke off as a rushing sound suddenly filled the air, followed by a loud crash.

Both girls spun round, and there in the fireplace – where only seconds earlier they had been standing – was a huge mound of soot and rubble.

Chapter 2

"The rooks probably disturbed something," said Sophie's dad as he peered up
the chimney, watched anxiously by his
wife and the two girls.

"I think it was a ghost," said Alice
excitedly. "I told you, didn't I, Sophie – I
said there would be a ghost."

Dad laughed, wiping soot from his

hands. "Well, if it is a ghost, he's being a bit of a pest because I've now got to call in a chimney sweep – I'd better go and look through the phone book and see if I can find one."

"It's a good job you girls weren't standing underneath," said Mum. Sophie noticed she looked quite pale. "You might have been seriously injured."

"Or even killed," said Alice. "Some ghosts are supposed to be friendly, but this one doesn't seem very friendly if he nearly got us killed, does he?"

"Well, he could be," said Sophie. "At least it didn't happen until after we moved out of the way."

"I think it's time you stopped all this talk of ghosts," said Mum firmly. "Go into the sitting room and put on the television, and I'll bring you in some tea."

Later, after Dad had taken Alice to her home in Newport, Sophie went to her bedroom to do her homework. She loved her room. The large window overlooked the gardens at the side of the house and it had its very own fireplace, surrounded by dark green tiles and a mantelshelf for her favourite books. Her bed was covered with a patchwork quilt made by her mother, tiny hand-

stitched pieces of material from every dress or skirt that Sophie had ever worn, while on her desk beneath the window, coloured clay pots made by her father held her pencils, pens and rulers.

Sophie stood for a moment before the window, watching the dusk as it settled on the garden, covering the lawns and hedges just like the quilt that covered her bed. The house was quiet and the

only sound to be heard from the garden was an occasional cawing from the tops of the trees as the rooks settled down for the night. Drawing the curtains, Sophie sat down at her desk and took some books from her school bag. Her homework was to finish the Victorian valentine card that she had started in class.

She worked steadily for about half an hour and was just putting the finishing touches to a bunch of violets on the front of the card, when she became aware of a tapping sound. It seemed to be coming from the fireplace, and at first Sophie thought it must be one of the rooks on the roof, but when it went on for a long time and became more persistent she stood up and walked to the fireplace.

This one was much smaller than the inglenook downstairs, and when Sophie tried to look up the chimney she found she couldn't see very far as it was too narrow.

The tapping noise continued and Sophie grew rather uneasy. It was a strange noise, not really the sort of noise a bird would make. She tried to ignore it, concentrating instead on the rich, deep purple of the violets' petals.

Tap tap tap. Tap tap tap, the noise went on. It was as if someone was trying to tell her something. In the end Sophie could bear it no longer and, throwing down her colouring pen, she picked up the card and ran out of the room and downstairs.

Mum and Dad were in the kitchen. It was warm and bright and safe in there. Mum was ironing and Dad was sitting at the table poring over his account books.

Mum looked up. "There you are. I was just coming to find you," she said. "Finished your homework?"

"Nearly." Sophie produced the card and showed it to her mother.

"That's lovely," said Mum admiringly. "Her drawing really has improved, hasn't it, Patrick?"

"Eh?" Dad looked up from the table. "Oh, yes," he said when he saw the card. "That's very good, love – I like pansies."

"They aren't pansies!" said Sophie indignantly. "They're violets. It's a Victorian valentine card. Miss Richardson said after she's seen them we can bring them home and give them to our valentine."

"So who's your valentine?" said Dad with a grin.

"I haven't got one," said Sophie. "'Spect I'll give it to you."

"Well, that's nice…" Dad laughed. "By the way, love, the chimney sweep is coming first thing in the morning."

"Oh, I shall be at school!" said Sophie. "I wanted to watch."

"You'll probably see him," said Mum as she folded the ironing board. "He said he'd be here before eight o'clock."

"There's a funny tapping noise coming from the chimney in my bedroom," said Sophie. "I don't like it – it's spooky."

"It'll be those blessed rooks nesting," said Dad.

"You only think it's spooky because of Alice and all her talk about ghosts," said Mum with a laugh.

"Well, there won't be anything to worry about after tomorrow," said Dad. "Sooty Attrill will put paid to any little games those pesky rooks might be up to in our chimneys."

"Who?" laughed Sophie.

"Sooty Attrill," repeated Dad with a straight face, "the chimney sweep."

"That can't be his real name," giggled Sophie.

"He didn't say it wasn't," said Dad.

Chapter 3

Sophie heard the noises again in the night. Tap tap tap. Tap tap tap, but followed this time by a swishing noise that reminded her of the sound someone would make if they were sweeping a yard with one of those huge witches' brooms. Somehow the thought of witches was even worse than the thought of ghosts, and in the end Sophie pulled the quilt over her head to shut out the strange noises.

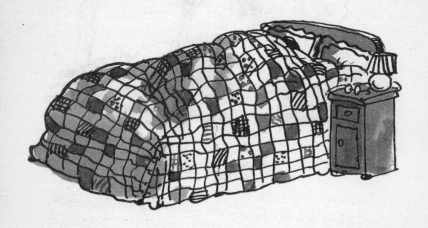

Eventually she must have gone back to sleep for when she awoke it was daylight and the room was quiet, which was surprising because outside in the trees the rooks were making a fearful din. Sophie was about to snuggle down under her quilt again when she heard the crunching of car tyres on the gravel.

Quickly she jumped out of bed, hopped across the room to the window and drew back the curtains. Down on the drive was a yellow van with the words *S. Attrill. Chimney Sweep* on the side. A man dressed in dark blue overalls was lifting a machine from the back of the van.

There was a crisp white frost and the grass and shrubs in the garden sparkled so much it was as if hundreds of diamonds were hidden in their depths. In the trees, the birds' nests, surrounded by bare branches, looked like huge black spiders against the icy blue sky. Sophie dressed and hurried downstairs, anxious not to miss anything the chimney sweep might do. She found him setting up his machine (which looked like a huge vacuum cleaner) and sealing off the inglenook fireplace.

"Hello," he said cheerfully when he caught sight of her. "Come to watch?"

Sophie nodded, wondering again if his name really was Sooty. She longed to ask but didn't quite dare. He didn't look at all sooty. In fact, for a chimney sweep his clothes really were quite clean.

"Will it make a mess?" she said at last.

"Shouldn't do," Sooty Attrill laughed. "Not these days."

"It used to, didn't it?" Sophie continued, "In the olden days. Grandma says when she was a little girl all the furniture had to be covered over with old sheets on the day the chimney sweep came."

"That's right." Sooty plugged in the vacuum machine. "And even further back than that, do you know what they used to do?"

Sophie shook her head.

"The sweeps used to train little boys to go up the chimneys with brushes to clean them."

"Little boys?" whispered Sophie.

"Yep." Sooty nodded then scratched his head through a thick layer of grey hair. "No older than you they were, some of them. Cruel it was really. There's a story about one of them in these parts, only a little lad he were. Somebody Gray his name was, he lived round here. Still, this won't do – I must get on." He switched on the machine and turned back to the fireplace.

Sophie had to leave for school long before the sweep had finished cleaning the many chimneys of Westcombe Manor, but when she returned late that afternoon, the yellow van had gone.

"That should put paid to any more noises or falls of soot," said Dad when they sat down to supper.

"Had the rooks built nests in the chimney pots?" asked Mum.

"Sooty Attrill said not. Apparently there was no sign of any twigs or anything," said Dad, "but I think he must have been mistaken – I can't think what else it could have been."

There were no noises that night when Sophie went to bed, but very early next morning she was awoken by something – the tapping sound again, she thought. She lay wide-eyed on her back for a long time, her heart thumping, but when everything remained quiet she thought she must have heard the noises in a dream.

It was Saturday, and as she didn't have to go to school she tried to go back to sleep, but she couldn't. In the end she got out of bed, opened her bedroom door and peered out at the landing. It really was very early; the lamp her mother left burning at night on top of the chest of drawers was still alight and her parents' bedroom door was tightly shut.

Feeling thirsty, Sophie padded downstairs and into the kitchen. It was almost dawn and the cold, grey light crept through the high window and under the blinds. Shivering slightly, Sophie opened the fridge and took out a carton of orange juice. She poured some juice into her mug, then carefully, so as not to spill it, she went back down the passage into the hall. She was about to climb the stairs again when she noticed that the door to the dining room was ajar. She stopped, and pushing the door fully open, went into the room.

It was even colder inside and Sophie could see delicate, fern-like frost patterns on the window panes. She crossed the room and holding her mug tightly, reached out her other hand and began tracing the patterns with one finger.

Beyond the window the gardens appeared almost ghostly in their grey-white shroud of frost. Later, when the sun rose, they would glitter and sparkle but until then they really looked quite spooky.

Sophie shivered again and turned away from the window. Her bed would still be warm, especially if she burrowed down under the patchwork quilt. She wasn't sure why she glanced towards the inglenook fireplace, and only knew that when she did, the shock of what she saw almost made her drop the mug of orange juice.

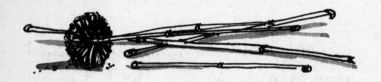

Chapter 4

A boy was sitting on the ledge inside the inglenook, a boy of about her own age. He was sitting very still – his thin arms hugging his knees, which were drawn up under his chin – and he was watching her.

"Oh!" Sophie gasped. "You made me jump. Who are you?" she said when he didn't move. "What are you doing there?"

He didn't answer immediately, just carried on staring at Sophie with dark, sad eyes.

He was pale, she noticed, very pale – his eyes huge beneath the brim of a soft black cap that he wore pulled well down over his forehead.

"How did you get in here?" Sophie's gaze flew to the frost-patterned windows, but they were closed and tightly fastened.

"I tried knocking." The boy straightened his legs, easing himself off the shelf. "But no one answered."

Sophie stared at him. Knocking? Had it been him making all those noises? She knew it was rude to stare but she couldn't help it; neither could she help but notice how thin he was and how ragged his clothes were. His wrists stuck out from the frayed cuffs of a jacket that was several sizes too small, while below his tattered trousers his knees were grazed and red. He was wearing sturdy black boots but he didn't appear to have any socks and his thin legs looked blue with cold.

"Everyone is in bed," Sophie replied, "that's why no one answered – but you still haven't told me who you are."

The boy's eyes darkened slightly. "I'm Valentine," he said.

Sophie stared at him in astonishment. Valentine?

Then she remembered. It was February 14th. Saint Valentine's Day. Did the boy mean he was *her valentine*?

Sophie wasn't sure she wanted him to be. He was so strange. His clothes were so ragged, and he was dirty – a black streak on his cheek, others on his legs, and his hands looked filthy … but … but… Sophie suddenly felt ashamed for even thinking these things. Perhaps he was poor, perhaps his parents had no money. She brought her gaze back to his face and saw he was smiling. It was a sad but beautiful smile.

She took a deep breath. "I'm Sophie," she said.

"I know," the boy replied.

How did he know? She eyed him warily as he stepped from the inglenook into the room. He began prowling around, touching things; the table, the backs of the chairs, the brass handles on the glass doors of the bookcase. He moved like a cat, one of those thin, grey cats you see in dark alleyways in towns.

He moved to the window and Sophie could see wisps of dark hair escaping from the black cap.

"Have you brought me a card?" she asked after a moment.

He turned and frowned at her. "Card?" he said.

"Yes. We've been making them all week at school…" she paused. "Haven't you?" she added curiously.

The boy shook his head. "Don't go to school," he said wiping his mouth with the back of his hand.

"Don't go to school?" Sophie was amazed. Everyone she knew had to go to school. "Why not?"

He shrugged. "Because I have to work."

"But that's terrible..." Sophie began, then she stopped, wondering if he had to work because he was so poor.

"I'm an apprentice," the boy said proudly.

"Whatever's that?" Sophie was bewildered.

"I'm learning to be a chimney sweep."

Sophie stared at him. Sooty Attrill had said something about boys learning to be chimney sweeps.

"I've come to give you a warning," the boy said, staring back at her.

"A warning?" Sophie frowned.

"Yes," said the boy, "and you must take notice. If you don't, your life may be in danger."

"Whatever do you mean?" Sophie's eyes widened in fear.

"This chimney," the boy indicated the inglenook. "It runs up through your bedroom, doesn't it?"

Sophie nodded. "Yes, but—"

"It isn't safe," the boy interrupted her. "It could come crashing down at any time."

"Oh!" Sophie's hand flew to her mouth. "How do you know?" she asked.

"I know this chimney well," the boy said, turning and gazing up at the inglenook. "I've cleaned it many times and I know that now, it isn't safe. You must tell your parents so that they can have it repaired or taken down altogether. You must do that, Sophie. You will, won't you?" He turned back to her.

"Oh, yes," she said, "yes, I will. Of course I will."

"I have to go now," he said, drawing himself upright and straightening his thin shoulders.

"Oh, no," Sophie cried. "Please don't go yet. Can't you stay a while? Have some breakfast with me. Then we could play."

The boy looked wistful, as if he would like nothing better than to have a good breakfast. "What would we play?" he asked doubtfully.

"Anything you like," said Sophie. "What are your favourite games?"

He frowned. "I used to play chase with my brother, but that was a long time ago ... and hide-and-seek..."

"All right," said Sophie quickly, "we'll play hide-and-seek."

The boy hesitated then he said, "No, I have to go, but maybe … maybe I can come back later…"

"Wait a moment," said Sophie. "Don't go yet. I have something for you," she added, afraid he was going to disappear as suddenly as he had arrived. "Please wait, it's in my room. I won't be long."

In her bedroom Sophie had just found the valentine card when she heard her parents' bedroom door open, then the sound of her father as he went down the stairs. She picked up the card and, hoping that the boy wouldn't think the violets were too cissy, she ran lightly back down the stairs.

Her father was in the hall about to unbolt the front door.

"Daddy," she called from the stairs, and he stopped and looked up at her.

"Hello, sweetheart," he said. "You're up early."

"I was up earlier than this," Sophie replied.

"Were you now?"

"Yes," said Sophie. "We have a visitor."

"Visitor?" Dad frowned.

"Yes, he's in the dining room."

"Who is it?" Her father looked startled.

"I think he works for Sooty Attrill," said Sophie. "He said he had to warn us about the chimney."

"Chimney? What chimney?"

"The big one," said Sophie, "the inglenook. He says it's not safe, that it could come crashing down."

"Good gracious!" Dad looked thoroughly alarmed. "I'd better have a word with him." He turned towards the dining room.

Sophie wanted to stop him, wanted to

give the boy her card first, but she didn't want to tell Dad that the boy had said he was her valentine. She was afraid he might laugh. Instead, she followed her father slowly as he hurried ahead into the dining room.

As she entered the room, Dad looked over his shoulder at her. "So where is he?" he said.

Sophie's gaze flew to the inglenook fireplace – but it was empty.

Chapter 5

"But he was here," said Sophie in bewilderment. "I was talking to him," she added when she caught sight of her father's expression.

"Are you sure this wasn't just one of your make-believe games?" asked Dad.

"I don't play those games any more," said Sophie indignantly.

"Hmm, well." Her father turned to go out of the dining room.

"But what are you going to do about the chimney?" Anxiously Sophie followed him to the kitchen.

"What do you want me to do?" Dad shrugged and smiled and Sophie knew he didn't believe her.

"The boy said the chimney wasn't safe – it's dangerous, Daddy!" she cried.

Can YOU read four Young Hippo books?

The Young Hippo is sending a special prize to everyone who collects any four of these stickers, which can be found in Young Hippo books.

This is one sticker to stick on your own Young Hippo Readometer Card!

Collect four stickers and fill up your Readometer Card

There are all these stickers to collect too!

Get your Young Hippo Readometer Card from your local bookshop, or by sending your name and address to:

Young Hippo Readometer Card Requests, Scholastic Children's Books, 6th Floor, Commonwealth House, 1-19 New Oxford Street, London WC1A 1NU

Offer begins March 1997

This offer is subject to availability and is valid in the UK and the Republic of Ireland only.

Crack-Back® Plus

fasson®

Removable

Crack-Back® Plus

fasson®

Removable

Crack-Back® Plus

fasson®

Removable

Crack-Back® Plus

fasson®

Removable

Crack-Back® Plus

fasson®

Removable

Crack-Back® Plus

fasson®

Removable

"Come on, Sophie," said her father, "that chimney's been there a long time…"

"I know, that's why it isn't safe. Please Daddy, please, you have to do something about it."

Her father stared at her and for one long, dreadful moment Sophie thought he still didn't believe her. She was just wondering desperately what else she could do, when he tugged gently at his lower lip and said, "Tell you what, I'll give Sooty Attrill a ring and see what he says about it."

Sophie watched in an agony of suspense as her father found Sooty Attrill's number and dialled. He waited a moment, then muttered, "No one there, it's the answer-phone."

"Oh, no!" Sophie groaned, then listened as her father left their number and asked Sooty to ring them back.

"That's all I can do for the moment, sweetheart," he said.

"I am telling the truth, Daddy," said Sophie.

"Okay," said Dad. "I believe you." He paused. "I wonder why Sooty didn't say anything when he was here. On the other hand," he scratched his head, "now I come to think of it, your mum and I weren't here when he finished, we'd gone into Newport to the supermarket."

"Well, there you are then," said Sophie excitedly. "That's why he sent the boy to tell you." She hesitated, "He said he was an … an … appren…"

"Apprentice?" said Dad with a frown.

"Yes, that's it," said Sophie, "an apprentice."

Dad shook his head then began to fill the kettle for his early-morning cup of tea.

Sophie wandered out of the kitchen and back into the dining room. The boy *had* been there, she thought, gazing

round the room. Right there in the inglenook fireplace. She hadn't imagined it. She knew she hadn't. She had spoken to him, could describe him in detail, from the soft, black cap he wore to his red, grazed knees and the thin wrists that stuck out from the ragged sleeves of his jacket.

But where was he now? He had disappeared in the short time she had been upstairs. Maybe he had heard Dad and had been afraid. But how had he got out of the house? The front door had still been bolted, probably the back door as well. Come to that, how had he got in? She stared at the windows, all fastened, as no doubt were the others in the house in this cold weather. Her gaze left the window and came to rest on the inglenook fireplace. That was where he had been when she had come into the room.

Slowly she walked to the fireplace and stepped inside. It felt cold, slightly damp and smelt of soot. She stared up into the blackness of the chimney. Sooty Attrill had said that in the olden days little boys had to climb the chimneys and sweep the soot away with a brush. Sophie suddenly shivered and was about to step out into the room again when she glanced up one more time and her gaze came to rest on the shelf where the boy had been sitting. At the same moment she realized she was still carrying the card – the valentine card with the purple violets.

She hesitated for only a moment, then standing on tiptoe she pushed the card on to the shelf. The boy had wanted to come back and play. Maybe he would. If he did he would find the card and know she had left it for him.

After breakfast Sophie went shopping in Newport with her mother. They were on the way back to the car park when they met Alice with her mother. They stopped to chat and Alice's mother invited Sophie back to lunch.

"I'll run her home later," she said.

Any other time Sophie would have loved the idea. But today was different. Today she just wanted to go home to see if her new friend had come back, and to make sure the chimney was made safe.

"That would be lovely," Mum was saying. "I worry that Sophie gets lonely where we live. There don't seem to be any other children nearby for her to play with. I'll see you later, darling."

To Sophie's dismay, Mum waved her hand and was gone.

"Come on, Sophie," said Alice. "We only live over there – on the other side of the park."

Miserably, she trailed after Alice and her mother.

"Guess what," said Alice excitedly. "I had a valentine card!"

"Did you?" said Sophie.

"Yes," Alice sighed. "I know it was from Jason Biddleton – it didn't say it was, but I know. I sent him mine. I'll die when I see him on Monday at school – I just know I will. Did you get a card, Sophie?"

Sophie shook her head and Alice's mum smiled. "Never mind," she said. "You haven't been here all that long, have you, Sophie?"

Alice talked non-stop about Jason Biddleton all the way across the park to her house. Sophie longed to tell her about her valentine but was afraid Alice wouldn't believe her.

Before lunch they played on Alice's computer, then while they were sitting at the kitchen table eating sausages and chips Alice suddenly said, "Did the chimney sweep come?"

Sophie nodded.

"Who did you have?" asked Mrs Jupe.

"Er, Mr Attrill," replied Sophie. She didn't like to say Sooty.

She needn't have worried because Mrs Jupe said, "Oh, you mean Sooty. I know Sooty Attrill well."

"Do you know his app ... apprentice?" asked Sophie on a sudden impulse. She found herself holding her breath as she waited for a reply.

"Apprentice?" Mrs Jupe frowned. "No," she shook her head, then said, "I don't think chimney sweeps have apprentices these days."

"They used to," said Alice. "We did all about that last year at school, before you came, Sophie. Miss Richardson told us all about the little chimney boys. There's a stone about one of them in the park. We passed it just now, didn't we, Mum?"

Mrs Jupe nodded. "Yes, it's a memorial stone. We'll take Sophie over there again after lunch, Alice, and show her."

Chapter 6

The stone was in one corner of the park against a wall, beneath the trees.

"Here it is." Alice led the way across the grass.

Sophie, following more slowly with Mrs Jupe, did not reach the stone until Alice had read it.

"Oh, look," said Alice. "I'd forgotten

that was his name."

"So had I," said Mrs Jupe, bending down. "Isn't that strange, today of all days. Look, he was only ten years old. He couldn't have had any fun in his life.

Thank goodness they don't make young boys do that sort of thing today."

Sophie stared down at the stone as Alice read the inscription aloud.

"'To the Memory of Valentine Gray, the Little Sweep. January the 5th A.D. 1822. In the 10th Year of his Age.

"'In Testimony of the General Feeling For Suffering Innocence…'"

There was more, and Alice read on, but Sophie didn't hear. All she could do was stare at the name.

Valentine Gray.

Her valentine.

She couldn't wait to get home – had to force herself to be patient, to be polite to Alice and her mother, to thank them for having her to lunch. But at last they were in Mrs Jupe's car and soon were turning into the large gates of Westcombe Manor.

"It really is the most beautiful old house," said Mrs Jupe as the manor came into view. "Seen any ghosts yet?"

Sophie was saved from answering as Mrs Jupe suddenly broke off then exclaimed, "What's that scaffolding for?"

Sophie leaned forward and saw two men lifting scaffolding poles from the back of a lorry.

"I don't know," she said, "but I think I can guess."

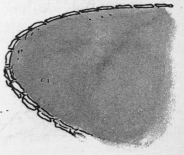

As the car came to a halt before the front door Sophie scrambled out of the back seat, and not waiting for Alice or her mother, ran into the house. She met her father in the hall.

"Daddy...?" she cried.

"Hello, sweetheart," he said. "You were quite right about that chimney."

"Did you speak to Sooty Attrill?"

"No." Her father shook his head. "I got the builders in and they tested the big chimney stack…"

"And...?" breathed Sophie.

"Some of the brickwork is loose outside. It's extremely dangerous, could have toppled at any time... Oh, hang on a minute, the phone's ringing!" He turned and went back into the kitchen.

Sophie stood very still; she could hear her mother outside, talking to Alice and Mrs Jupe. She glanced towards the kitchen where Dad was talking on the phone.

With her heart beating so hard she was afraid it might burst, she walked slowly into the dining room. The last of the afternoon sunshine highlighted the sheen on the polished table, but the inglenook fireplace was deep in shadow. Sophie crossed the room and stepped inside. Surprisingly, this time, it didn't feel cold. Standing on tiptoe she reached up to the shelf and felt along its surface.

It was empty. The boy, Valentine, had come back for her card! Sophie stood for a moment gazing up at the shelf.

She was about to turn away, when out of the corner of her eye she caught sight of something on the floor of the inglenook. Bending down she picked it up, and as Dad came into the dining room she just had time to thrust it into the pocket of her anorak.

There was a puzzled expression on Dad's face. "That was Sooty Attrill on the phone," he said. "I asked him about the chimney being unsafe and he said he didn't know anything about it – that it had seemed all right to him when he had cleaned it."

"Did he say anything else?" asked Sophie.

"You mean about the boy?" said Dad. "Well, that was the most extraordinary part of all. When I mentioned the boy, he didn't know what I was talking about.

He doesn't have anyone working for him and never has had – so goodness knows who it was you saw, Sophie. Mind you, it was a good thing, whoever he was, because it seems he has prevented what could have been a very nasty accident."

At that moment Alice burst into the room and Dad went off, shaking his head.

"There you are, Sophie," said Alice. "I was just showing your mum the valentine card that Jason sent me. We've got to go now."

Sophie walked back into the hall, then stood with her mother and watched as the Jupes' car disappeared down the drive.

"Did you mind not having a valentine?" asked Mum, putting her arm round Sophie's shoulders.

"No." Sophie shook her head, but at the same time slipped her hand inside her anorak pocket.

"There's always next year," said Mum.

Sophie smiled. Somehow, she thought, as they turned to go back into the house, she didn't think she'd have to wait that long before she saw her valentine again – because even if he couldn't come back to play, surely he would have to come back to collect his cap.

The End

Valentine Gray was a real chimney sweep and his memorial stone can be seen in a park at Church Litten, Newport, Isle of Wight.